Murder in
Dartmouth Park

By Tim Lewis

Also by Tim Lewis:

Murder in Belgrave Square,
      The first book of this series.

The rest of the series, coming soon:
      Murder in Queen's Park
      Death on the Docks
      A Killer in the House

DEDICATIONS

Kymberlie Ingalls

To my editor. You have kept me honest and "on point" throughout this project. You have my sincere gratitude for your love of writing and your uncanny ability to spot my short-comings. Meet me at any pub, restaurant, or coffee shop dear friend. I'm buying.

Thanks to David Prendergast, freelance designer, for creating a cover, which captures the essence of this story.
Find him at ebookscoversdesign.com

Introduction

January 1892:

Scotland Yard Detective Edward Willoughby and his team of police officers have arrested the Duchess of Manchester for the murder of her husband, and for hiring a contract assassin to kill his mistress. The killer is still at large.

Ronald Alexander's Garment Factory Targets:

1.   The Principle Owners:
    1.   Langley Smythe (principle, 76%)
    2.   Harley Winthorpe (principle, 13%)
    3.   Harold Lawton (principle 7%)
    4.   ~~Luella Walford aka Lady Manchester (principle, 4%) In Prison~~
        1.   Arrested for Murder of her husband, and for hiring a contract killer to murder his mistress.

2.   Management:
    1.   John Collingworth
    2.   Janet Englert
    3.   Reginald Naughton
    4.   Neville Garner

One

25 January 1892, 0213:

"Bloody Arsehole", John Collingworth muttered as he left the pub. The yellow rectangle went dark as the door closed, and night once again became bluish-black.

He stepped into the night, double-wrapped the knit scarf around his neck and buttoned his coat. He glanced at his skinned-up knuckles as he stuffed his hands into his leather gloves. *That bugger will think twice before arguing wi' me.*

The wind continued, now that the snow stopped falling. Winter clawed its way inside his clothes. Still, he welcomed the winter nights. No one would bother him as he walked home.

The large man trudged, bending into the wind, hugging the buildings facing away from the breeze. Snow coated the bricks and windows and created dirty white mounds in door stoops. The buildings offered precious little comfort from the wind, but precious little was better than none at all. His breath left him in large clouds.

The brick and stone canyon reminded John of Newgate prison. *A lifetime ago,* he thought.

He turned and entered Dartmouth Park, a wide, grassy field with no cover. He held an unlit cigarette as he approached a man in an overcoat.

"Got a light?" he asked his fellow late night venturer.

"Certainly." The man held out a lit match. The flame revealed the stranger's kind, disarming face. A man you would never notice in a crowd.

"Thank ye," John said.

"My pleasure," the stranger responded.

Collingworth turned and continued along the path. The stranger spun. In an instant a blade sliced its way through the scarves and across his neck. Blood spurted out at a wide angle. The last thing he heard was "For my children."

He died before his head hit the gravel.

25 January 1892, 0542, Highgate Cemetery:

"Hey you," the policeman said, as he paused on the sidewalk of Swan Lane. "You can't be here."

The man leaned against the heavy oak doors at the cemetery's main entrance. A blanket of fog billowed around him. The country estate-looking granite structure loomed large, the stone steps wet from the early morning fog.

Something queer about him, the bobby thought, motioning for a second officer a few yards away for assistance. Together they approached the man-statue.

"Sir," the clean-shaved junior officer said. "You need to go sleep it off."

The second officer used his nightstick to tap the gent on the shoulder, and the body fell onto the stone porch. A gloved hand turned the man over, revealing a slit throat and a blood-soaked scarf and coat. The eyes told a story. The lifeless orbs complemented the shocked expression. A note was attached to the man's lapel.

"Jesus, Mary and Joseph," the officer said. "We need a detective." He pulled his whistle and blew a long, continuous note.

25 January 1892, 0755, Scotland Yard:

Cadet Peterson sat down with a deep sigh. Detective Edward Willoughby's Scotland Yard office, with its temporary conversion to a crime center, surrounded him. Two blackboards were crammed with scrawls, and two cork bulletin boards were covered with documents and notes. The desk and tables were piled with folders.

"I can't connect everything," he said. "Ronald Alexander doesn't appear in every scenario."

"He doesn't have to," Detective Willoughby said. "We're not proving anything at this time to a reasonable certainty. What we *are* proving is the possibility of his involvement with the Alice Stormgrove murder."

"And if we prove it?" Cadet Brown said. "We still don't know where he is."

"True." Patrolman Andreason, the fourth member Edward's team, took another puff from his pipe. "But we can put his description out to every station in greater London so at least every copper can be aware. Perhaps we'll get lucky and find him."

"Luck?" Peterson said, smoothing his hair for the hundredth time. "You're counting on providence?"

"Sometimes you make your own fortune, Cadet," Edward said. "Suppose you want to increase your chance of winning a lottery. What would you do?"

"Purchase more tickets," Brown said.

"Correct. The more eyes looking for Ronald Alexander, the better our chances are of finding him." Edward puffed on his own pipe and then added, "Luck."

"On the other hand," Andreason said, "We don't want to waste our time looking for someone who is not involved."

"So how do we proceed?" Peterson asked.

"We don't have enough evidence to go to my superiors and ask for resources which may or may not be needed. So we gather more evidence." Edward glanced at the clock. "Time for work, gentlemen."

The four policemen grabbed their coats and hats in preparation for entering London's winter. Edward paused and looked inside his bowler before placing it upon his head.

"Detective Willoughby?"

"Yes, Cadet Peterson?"

"I've seen you stare into your hat several times since this investigation started. Why is that?"

"Oh?" Edward said, raising an eyebrow. "Oh, that. It's a warning. A reminder to me of why we do what we do."

"I don't understand."

"Look here," Edward said, removing his hat and pointing at the lining. "There—it's an earring from a victim who never received justice. She deserved better. I arrived in court, confident we would achieve a guilty verdict. We didn't. It reminds me to do better. So far it's the only case I have ever lost.

"We must be excellent. Perfect, if we intend to put criminals in prison where they belong. Most important, we protect the innocent, wherever they are."

"And with that lecture to begin our morning," Andreason said, "let's be off."

25 January 1892, 0815:

"How ye be this morning, Edward?" Detective Sergeant Albert Johnson looked over his raised reception desk at New Scotland Yard. His full black beard was combed, and his starched shirt looked as if it would crack if he bent over. Edward Willoughby's team exited the stairwell and headed toward the front door.

"About to join the land of the living, I believe," Edward said.

"In that case, I must redirect you to the land of the dead. A body at Highgate Cemetery begs your expertise."

"How so?"

"The body was posed, to appear to be awake." Albert lowered his voice and handed a paper to Edward. "The throat has been slashed. Oh, there's a note for you on the body."

Edward stared into the sergeant's eyes for a moment, hoping he was joking. He sighed as he read the offered telegram. "Well, we're dressed for outside. Thank you, Detective Sergeant Johnson," Edward said, jamming his hands into his gloves. He turned to his team. "Peterson, hail us a cab. We're off to Highgate Cemetery."

25 January 1892, 0855, Highgate Cemetery:

The horse and carriage stopped in front of the main entrance to London's "most magnificent final resting place". Edward and his team stepped onto the walk.

The fog still covered the graves and headstones. Water dripped everywhere. The light breeze swirled the gray clouds around the mausoleums and ornate headstones.

"Detective Willoughby?" A young policeman said, snapping to attention.

"I am Willoughby, and you would be?" Edward noted the blue fingers. *He must be freezing.*

"Foot Patrolman Daniels. Please follow me."

A dozen uniformed bobbies kept the growing crowd back from the entrance to the cemetery. Daniels led the investigation team to the left side of the main gate, where a body lay on its back.

Edward crouched beside the man. The face was familiar, and he studied the features. *Yes, it is you, John,* he thought. *A few new scars, but your face has not changed. You got what you deserved at last.* The detective pulled out his notepad.

"John Collingworth," Edward said. "One of the Garment Seven."

"I see," said Andreason. "What role did he play in the fire and tragedy?"

"He locked the doors and kept the gates closed, making escape impossible. The gate guard. He's hated by everyone he meets. No one likes this man."

"Then our suspect list just became very long."

"The note is with this body…curious."

"Sir?"

"The previous murder. The note was not with Alice Stormgrove," Edward said as he sniffed the cold air. "We had to dig for it."

"Quite right," Andreason answered. He looked at the envelope pinned to the lapel of John Collingworth's coat.

Edward leaned in and smelled the paper and retrieved a pair of tongs from his briefcase. He pulled the straight pin and picked up the envelope, which bore the words:

```
     For Detective Edward Willoughby
              Scotland Yard
```

He broke the seal with a pen knife and read the card:

```
         It continues
```

"Wot continues?" Patrolman Daniels said.

"The pursuit continues, Officer Daniels," Edward said. "The chase."

Two

"Disturbing the crime scene, Detective?" Coroner Waddington fitted his spectacles over his ears. He peered at the body of John Collingworth, a clinical look, beginning at the head, ending at the feet.

"Hopefully not," Edward replied. "We have not moved the body, but have rummaged what pockets are available to us."

"Hmpf." Waddington looked over his glasses. "Trying to find another note?"

"It was pinned to the victim's lapel."

Waddington glanced at the note then walked around the body once more. "Did ye notice the mud on his shoes?"

"I did."

"There's no mud near the gate, and there are no muddy footprints leading to the body. He was carried here. This is not the scene of the crime."

"I surmised as much. When you are back in the morgue, will you be able to find where the mud came from?"

"Possibly…possibly not. You need to widen your search."

"Kentish Station has all available policemen doing just that. We'll be interviewing John Collingworth's widow later this morning."

"John Collingworth? Are you certain, Edward?"

"Positive. I spent a year in court staring at his smug face."

"Not so smug now. Hmmm…time to roll the body."

Two of Waddington's assistants grasped the body and rolled it over. The coroner pulled John's gloves off and studied the hands at length. He looked back and forth at them, over and over.

"Do you see something, sir?" Edward said.

"Possibly. The skinned knuckles suggest he was recently in a fight…not so unusual for our victim. The fresh burn mark, right here, interests me." The coroner pointed at the first and second fingers. "He had a cigarette in this hand when he was killed."

"He was comfortable," Edward said. "He did not expect to be attacked."

"A friend did this perhaps?"

"He had no friends. I'm thinking a stranger. Someone you would pass on the street and never give a second glance."

"Anything else you need here, Edward?" Waddington studied the body. "I need to get the body back to the morgue."

"One thing, sir," Edward sighed. "A rough time of death, if you would be so bold."

"Six hours, eight at most." Waddington pushed at the scars on the victim's fingers. "Perhaps less."

"Thank you, sir. We have some work to do."

"I'll keep you posted."

"As will I. Good day, sir."

Willoughby walked to his team, who were discussing the scene. Officer Andreason was furiously taking notes.

"We need to find where this victim was killed," Peterson said.

"We will have a chat with the Kentish Station Sergeant about that. Where are the discovering officers?" Edward asked.

"This way, Detective," a tall sergeant said. His red goatee was coated with morning dew. The team walked to two officers standing with another sergeant. "Detective Edward Willoughby, Officers O'Reilly and MacTavish."

Both officers snapped to attention.

"Good morning, gents," Edward eyed the two Bobbies carefully. "We'll have a few questions, and then you can be off to finish your paperwork. Who first noticed the victim?"

"That would be me, Clifton O'Reilly, patrolman from Kentish Station." The officer's red muttonchops wiggled when he spoke, and his mustache was carefully shaped to a thin line connecting to the corners of his jaw. His red eyes revealed exhaustion, a man long past the end of his shift.

"Very good. You understand the area and your patrol. How long would this gate be unobserved by you or one of your fellow officers?"

"Well, sir," the officer cleared his throat. "Fifteen minutes, twenty-five at most. MacTavish, you would concur?"

"Ah, yes," the younger officer said. "It's hard to say, since we don't use a watch to guide our patrols. Twenty-five minutes would be the most time away from the gate."

"Last question," Edward said. "Did ye notice any carriages or wagons loitering nearby?"

"No, sir," O'Reilly said.

"None since midnight," MacTavish added. "Only a cabbie parked in front of Wally's pub. I think he got a fare and ne're returned to the area."

"Thank you, sirs," Edward said. "Sergeant, any reports of stolen carts or cabs in the area?"

"Not yet, sir. We'll keep a lookout." The second sergeant said, rubbing his hands together.

"Thank you, Sergeant…"

"Masters, sir." Sergeant Masters said, ensuring his posture was perfect.

"Thank you, Sergeant Masters. Oh, we're finished here at Highgate, at least for the moment. I'll leave it to your men to return the area to the public."

"Thank you, sir," Masters said. "The city workers have been pressing us to allow them to clean up the area. We should have the preliminary paperwork finished by ten o'clock. Should we send it to Scotland Yard?"

"Actually, " Edward said, "Wire us at the Yard, and Cadet Brown will pop by to retrieve it, if that is all right with you."

"I'm Cadet Brown," He said, raising his hand.

"Brilliant. I'll make a note of it."

"Thank you, Sergeant. It looks like all of you could do with some rest and warmth."

"Indeed." Masters turned to his officers. "Lads, let's wrap this up and retire to the station."

25 January 1892, 1119, Dartmouth Park:

Two Bobbies walked the cross-pathway at Dartmouth Park. Their regular patrol traveled this route each morning, and they officially started on the far side.

Officer Richardson waited for Officer Norrington to tie his loose shoelace. Norrington looked a dozen feet down the path when he saw it. A bloody cigarette.

"Hullo, Bishop," and strode forward, his lace flapping wildly. He crouched, then looked beyond the cigarette. "My word. Look at that. Is that blood?" He pointed at a brown pool.

"I believe you're right." Richardson walked a few paces farther on. "Pardon me, but that's a lot of blood. Stay here, and I'll hurry back to the station." There's no way the victim walked away from this.

25 January 1892, 1331, Dartmouth Park:

"Too many footprints to know for certain," Andreason said, making notes in his book.

"Perhaps that is what the killer counted on," Edward commented. "But this area is so open. The risk of being seen would have been very good."

"Uh, Detective," Officer Norrington interrupted, "that may not be true."

"How so?" Edward asked, raising an eyebrow.

"The fog," Norrington straightened his coat. "I checked with the midnight shift, and the visibility would have been less than twenty five feet."

"Point taken. Then, not so risky. "

"Sir?" Norrington held a curious look. "These past nights there had been little fog. Until last night. A patient killer, perhaps?"

"Possibly." Edward wrote in his notebook, and the patrolman turned away. "Norrington?"

"Sir?"

"Good observations. If you think of anything else, let me know."

"Yessir." The officer smiled, stood a little taller and walked back to the rest of the policemen.

Three

Edward's second mug of coffee was growing cold, and he wandered toward the coffee pot for a refill of the brown swill. He had already assigned his regular cases to the other detectives in the cold case section, and he could now concentrate on the contract killer.

The wall clock arrived at nine o'clock as Officer Andreason led the two cadets onto the third floor of New Scotland Yard. A work area had already been set up with a large table and stacks of editions of the London Times.

"Gents," Edward began, "This is where good, solid police work begins. We're going to attempt to find out what caused Ronald Alexander to attempt to escape from prison. Further, we need to find out why he became a contract killer, and who would bear the brunt of his ire.

"Ronald Alexander escaped on 24 June, 1885. I captured him on 29 June of the same year, in Cardiff. His payment for escaping was to serve the remains of his sentence at Darlinghurst Gaol in Sydney, Australia. In front of us are the editions of The Times for six months preceding the escape. We are looking for anything involving any of Mr. Alexander's relatives, including his wife, whose maiden name was Wellsley."

"How long would he have taken to plan his escape?" Peterson said.

"He's a patient, brilliant soul," Edward said. "He could have planned it for months, years even."

"Shall we get started?" Andreason said. "If he's as patient as you say, shall we concentrate, beginning with six months before his escape? With one of us looking at each month, we should cover most of the papers by this afternoon."

The next hours involved the flipping of pages, the taking of copious notes, everyone concentrating on the task at hand. The area was quiet except for the noise of pages turning. This silence was disconcerting to Willoughby because it indicated the team had found nothing. He finished with the last newspaper in his stack and leaned back into his chair, thinking.

Andreason looked up from his last paper and shook his head. A few minutes later Cadet Brown indicated the same lack of success. They all watched Cadet Peterson, who held up one finger. He read an entire article from the last paper in his stack.

"Holy Jesus!" He breathed and reached for the top paper in the next stack. "The garment district fires. Remember how many were killed?" Willoughby, Andreason, and Brown leaned forward, watching the young cadet search. His fingers shook as he flipped to page six. "Yes. The management had locked the basement doors, which were the exits. No one was able to escape. Are we still looking for E.F.J. Alexander?"

"Yes," Edward said.

"I don't think he exists," Peterson's breath was halting, sporadic. "The letters might represent three people. Emmett, write this information down." Cadet Brown grabbed his notepad and fresh pencil.

Peterson flew through the pages, and it was not until a week after the fire they were able to release a list of victims. His index finger slid down the list of names, which were not in any order.

"Ellen Alexander, age fourteen," Peterson said, his finger continuing to scan the columns.

"John Alexander, age seventeen." Peterson's finger was relentless.

"Francis Alexander, age fifteen." Peterson looked up. "Ellen, Francis, and John Alexander: E.F.J. Alexander. His children died in the fire."

"We need to find out about his wife," Edward said, "but I fear she died earlier, causing the children to seek employment in the sweat shops. His family is dead. He has nothing left to live for, save revenge."

Four

"Pemberton Gardens, number 303, gents," the Bobby announced.

"Thank you, officer," Edward sighed. "We can take it from here."

The Bobby saluted and waited on the curb. Notification of a murder to the next of kin was reserved for detectives, who were trained in such matters. The first reaction of the spouse of the recently demised was also of paramount importance, in the event said spouse had a hand in the murder.

The weathered door had a broken knocker, so Edward Willoughby rapped the door with his bare knuckles. There was a shuffling inside, followed by muffled orders.

"Who is it?" a gruff woman's voice called out from the other side.

"Police," Edward said. "I'm trying to find the whereabouts of Olivia Collingworth."

"Well, ya found her."

"It would be much easier to chat if we came inside," Edward glanced at Andreason.

"Ya better have a badge, copper, because I have a club for ya otherwise."

Metal upon metal scraping sounds could be heard as the woman lid the bolt and opened the door a crack.

"Good enough?" Edward asked, showing his identification to the eye squinting at him.

"Oh all right," said the woman, who flung the door open as she turned back into the flat. "Come on in, and close the door behind ya."

She wore a gray shawl, and her gray hair ran halfway down her back. A black dress flowed to the floor, and her feet, clad in heavy wool socks, propelled her toward a coal fireplace on the far wall. Olivia Collingworth plopped into an overstuffed chair and picked up a cup of tea. Her wary eyes never left the policemen.

Cadet Brown closed the door, and Edward swung his head about the room. It was furnished with a mixture of luxury and poverty. A marvelous clock graced the mantel, while a crumbling rocker sat in a corner. The rug was new; yet the small cherry table by the sofa had seen one too many repairs.

Flanking the mantel clock were several photographs; yet no artwork adorned any of the walls. Heavy curtains covered all the windows. The room seemed as though it were night.

"Well, he ain't here, if that's what yer looking for," She said.

"If by 'he' you mean your husband John, no, I'm not looking for him." Edward studied the woman's squinting eyes, more curious now. She put her tea on a rickety table. "I'm afraid I have some bad news. Your husband was murdered this night past."

"What time would that 'ave been?" Olivia fidgeted with her blouse. "Because yesterday 'e left this trophy on me." She pulled up her sleeve, revealing fresh bruises. "Then the bastard wandered off to one of 'is favorite pubs."

"Do you remember which one?"

"No, and good riddance. The longer 'e's away from us, the better. Murdered, ya say?"

"Yes, murdered," Edward looked about the tiny flat. "You don't seem saddened by that fact."

"Have ya not been listenin'?" she said. "The man was a victimizer, a rogue, a scoundrel, and a wife-beater. Not that the magistrate would do anything about it. If I 'it 'im, I'd end up in the slammer, but if 'e puts me in the 'ospital, 'e pays me four pence and goes back to 'is work and 'is drink. No, Detective whatever-your-name-is, I am anything *but* saddened by me 'usband's demise."

"Besides yourself, do you know of anyone who might want to hurt your husband?"

"Open up me front door and look up and down the street. 'alf of them are going to feel sorry they didn't do 'im in. The other 'alf will praise whoever did. I doubt if six people show at the feunral."

"Would that include you? Would you be at the funeral?"

"You betcha." She took another sip of tea. "I want to make certain the bastard is dead."

"And where were you this night past or early this morning?"

"Right here, laddie, taking care of my young-ens."

"You have children?"

Olivia let out a shrill, loud whistle. Edward was unsuccessful in covering his ears. "Come out kiddies. It's only the police."

Four children filed into the room.

"This 'ere's Robbie, who's 12. Then there's Mary, 10; Sally, 8; and Clifford, who's 6," Olivia said. They all wore old clothes, and the oldest arranged his siblings by age.

"Stand up straight, Clifford," Robbie Collingworth told his younger brother. Robbie tried to hide the ripped sleeve on his plaid shirt. Clifford snapped out of his slouch. "The detective might want to ask you a question."

"Which one's the detective?"

"He's the one wearing the suit."

"Oh. Why?"

"'Cause that's what detectives wear."

"Oh. Why?"

"May I intercede on your behalf?" Edward asked.

"Be my guest," Robbie nodded.

"We wear street clothes so when we talk with someone like you, you feel more comfortable talking with someone like us."

"Oh. My dad ne'er 'it me," Clifford's eyes lit up. "If I did something bad, 'e would 'it Robbie."

"He would hit you?" Edward looked at the older boy.

"Yea." Robbie looked at his feet. "Sometimes I would give somepin back. Sometimes."

"Wait a minute," Olivia interrupted. "I just recognized ya. Yer that detective who tried to put my Johnnie away all those years ago. The garment factory fires. 'e only did what 'e was told, ya know."

"I won't mince words with you, Missus Collingworth. We both know what happened."

"Ya lost. That's what 'appened."

"Doesn't mean anyone won."

"Yer tryin' ta get me ta care aboot those cretins in the factries?" Her cheeks puffed as she spoke. "No chance in that."

"Nor would I expect it." Edward wrote in his notebook. "Since mourning seems out of the question, do you need anything?"

"Nuttin' from you, copper." Olivia looked at her four children. "You kids. Get ready for school. Now." Robbie stayed in the room

She seethed at Edward.

"One more question, Mrs. Collingworth. What was it your husband did for gainful employment?"

"Ya mean for work? 'e was night watchman for Penny Farthing, LLC."

"Still working for the garment industry, after all theses years. Interesting." Edward looked up from his notebook. "And you Mrs. Collingworth, what is it you do for gainful employment?"

"You're lookin' at it, sir. I take care of my young-ens, and that's a full-time job."

"Thank you, madam. Robbie." He tipped his hat. "I believe we can show ourselves out."

Five

The wind and fog buffeted the four policemen once they returned to the street.

"She's a pillar of the community, that one," Cadet Brown commented.

"We'll get no information from her," Cadet Peterson said.

"Did you notice, gentlemen?" Edward said, referring to his notes. "She never asked how she was going to make her way with her husband gone."

"I kept waiting for her to bring up the topic," Andreason said. "It leads me to believe she is certain she will be taken care of."

"And just where would she get enough money to support herself?" Cadet Brown asked.

"We long thought there was a bookkeeper," Edward said. "But we never found one. I doubt Olivia Collingworth fits that bill. A different position, perhaps?"

"How do we prove it?" Andreason said. "I doubt you'll get a magistrate to issue a search warrant for a newly widowed woman without something substantial to support it."

Edward walked until he was halfway down the block.

"We'll have to monitor her financial situation," Edward said. "Both internally and outwardly. See if she purchases new clothes for her or the children or does generous expenditures.

"Cadets, this will be your task." Edward eyed the two young men. "Go change into civilian clothes. Work out a schedule between the two of you, and stay on her for the next two weeks."

"Just two weeks?" Peterson said. "What if she does not move on the money?"

Edward scratched his chin. "Does she strike you as a patient woman?"

"No, sir," Peterson said. "So if she demonstrates new wealth or suspicious behavior, we note it and get that information to you?"

"Precisely," Edward said. He looked up and down the street. "There's a café on the corner there, along with a pub. Several other vendors are close enough for you to view the residence and be inconspicuous. Let's set each of you with a four-hour shift, which should cover all the daylight hours.

"After each shift you will review your notes with Officer Andreason and me. We will help you adjust your surveillance technique, so that you get better at your craft."

26 January 1892, 0731, New Scotland Yard Morgue:

"Throat slit, right to left, incision two inches deep, severing the carotid artery," Coroner Waddington recited from his notes. "An angry man does a wound *that* deep. Except for the depth, the wound is consistent with that sustained by Mary Stormgrove. We're looking for a left-handed killer. Is that what you wanted to hear, Edward?"

"Actually, I had hoped for something different, sir." Edward Willoughby mulled over the news that this might be a repeat killer-for-hire. "Now, I need to find what connects the two murders."

"Or what does not," Waddington said.

"Indeed." Edward sighed.

"The Earl of Manchester was shot," Andreason said.

"Yes," Edward replied, "but by his jealous wife. The problem we have, sirs, is half of London wanted John Collingworth dead." Edward took a long puff on his pipe, then let out a large cloud of smoke. "His wife said as much." He waved away some of the cloud. "Add the garment factory fire to the pile of reasons to wish him ill, and the list becomes large."

"Is she not a primary suspect?" Andreason asked.

"She interests me." Edward said. "There is not enough here to make her a suspect." Edward let out another gray cloud. "Not quite yet." He stroked his mustache, lost in thought.

26 January 1892, 0800:

The following morning found Cadet Brown taking his breakfast at the café then sauntering down the street, stopping to gaze into the windows. There was no movement from the Collingworth house, save the children going to school, and Mrs. Collingwood limiting her shopping to the local street vendors. Cadet Peterson took over the watching at lunch time, and at six o'clock he retreated to the comfort of New Scotland Yard.

"Nothing to report, sir," Cadet Peterson said.

"I wouldn't expect anything on the first day, lads. Keep at it for a week, and we'll see what happens." Edward made journal entries from both the cadets' logs.

The second day was equally uneventful. And the third. And the fourth.

Friday afternoon Peterson noted Mrs. Collingworth had left the house. He followed, hanging back perhaps a hundred yards. She sniffed and sampled several fruits, purchasing nothing.

On the corner Harold's Flowers banner covered half the block. She turned and stepped inside. Half an hour later, she returned with a brown package, wrapped with string. She hailed a cab and was gone.

Peterson made his way back to the Collingworth house and took up his watch from the café. He was just finishing his bagel when Mrs. Collingworth hobbled up the sidewalk, looking as challenging as ever. She opened the door to her flat, looked both ways up and down the street and disappeared inside. The cadet pulled out his pocket watch. Note: thirty-five minutes from the exit of the store to her return at her home.

31 January 1892, 1946:

"She didn't leave the rest of your shift?" Edward asked, leaning back in his chair.

"No, sir," Peterson answered. "I stayed an extra hour, and she stayed inside with her children."

"Stay on her, gents," Edward said. "Accurate notes. Times, dates, places. All of this will be presented as evidence in court. Are we clear?"

"Yessir," they answered as one.

The young cadets resumed their work with a purpose and observed the entire neighborhood. The comings and goings of everyone was documented. When the fishmonger arrived (No visual observation was necessary. The smell preceded the old man pushing his fish-laden cart, fresh from the docks.), the opening of the bakery, the curio shop, the bookstore, and the used clothing store hours were documented.

Friday, Mrs. Collingworth went to Harold's Flowers, exited with a bag, hailed a cab, and returned to her flat within thirty-five minutes. With the exception of this one excursion, the woman never ventured out of her neighborhood.

Six

1 February 1892, 1110:

"Cadets Brown and Peterson, I presume?" Charlie the cabbie eyed the young men. "Detective Willoughby says I'm supposed follow a cab from a particular address to wherever it goes. I'm to lay back so's the occupant isn't alerted to our presence. Is that about it?"

Cadets Brown and Peterson nodded in response.

"Well, then, git in so's we can git in position."

Charlie picked up Olivia Collingworth's cab after she exited the flower shop, and he did a masterful job of being discrete. They entered progressively more affluent neighborhoods until they saw it stop at an estate in Sunninghill. A footman met the cab, took the package, and handed Olivia Collingworth a thick envelope.

The Cadets observed Olivia Collingworth enter a bank five miles away from Sunninghill and one mile from her residence. A man in a suit greeted her and led her to the rear of the bank. Peterson wrote a description of the man:

"Tall man. Mutton chops, with long fringe. Short-cropped hair. Black suit, tailored and flared.

Red vest.

Yellow tie.

White shirt.

No smile.

All business.

Treated O.C. like a valued client…not like a woman without means."

She flagged a cab five minutes later. The driver let her out four blocks from her home.

1 February 1892, 1820:

"What were the dimensions of the envelope?" Edward asked.

"Slightly larger than a pound note and a bit over a half inch thick," Cadet Brown said. "It was bound with string; so the contents remain a mystery."

"She made no other stops?"

"No, sir," Peterson said. "Olivia shuffled home, resuming her posture as the recent poor widow. The trip took the usual thirty-five minutes to complete."

"We have her," Brown whispered.

"Not quite," Peterson replied. "It might not be enough to get a search warrant."

"But it *is* something."

"Indeed.   Indeed it is." Peterson looked at Detective Willoughby. "Isn't it?"

15 February 1892, 1945:

Edward Willoughby reviewed the notes of the two cadets. They sat breathless, awaiting for some reaction of the seasoned detective. Edward alternated between the two notebooks, Robert Andreason peering over his shoulder.

"All right, gents," Edward said, pushing the two journals toward the two young men, "you know the drill. Type this all up before you go home."

"But sir…" Cadet Brown started to object.

"It's procedure for a reason," Edward said. "Do the typing while this is still fresh."

"Yes, sir," Brown said.

"Oh, one more thing," Edward's mouth began an uncharacteristic smile which ran almost to his ears. "This is the quality of work I would expect of senior detectives. Well done!"

The two young men grabbed their notebooks and eagerly typed their notes into legible documents.

Edward and Robert conversed quietly while the cadets typed their reports. The clack-clack of steel upon ribbon upon paper was all that could be heard.   A half hour later they conversed, made corrections, and typed some more. Within an hour the reports were ready.

Willoughby reviewed both of the papers, then pushed them back to the cadets, who signed them.

"Go and celebrate, lads," Edward handed a pound note to Peterson. "The first round is on me. Officer Andreason and I have a bit more work to do, but we expect to see you here on time tomorrow."

"Thank you, sir," Cadet Peterson said. "Good night."

"Good night, sir," Cadet Brown added.

The two nearly floated out the door.

"Ah, youth," Andreason commented.

"Indeed," Edward said. "Promising, aren't they?"

"The best." Andreason smiled for a moment. "The very best indeed."

"Now, if we can convince one of our councilors to pursue a warrant, perhaps we can see what is so important at this particular bank." Edward looked toward Superintendent McCarthy's office. The lights were still on. "Special approval must be given to view protected bank information."

Edward scooped up the reports and walked toward the Superintendent's office.

Seven

"Do you believe she is the bookkeeper?" Superintendent McCarthy scratched his ample mutton chops as he leaned back from his desk.

"No sir. She does not have the head for it. She is only a bag lady," Edward said. "At the very least, the cash, if that is what this is, goes nowhere without an accounting of the amounts."

"Well, let's see what councilor Beachcroft says about this request," McCarthy said. He stared out the window, smoke from the pipe trailing off toward the glass. "I'll have an answer for you shortly, Edward."

"Thank you, sir," Edward closed the door and walked toward his desk. Andreason looked up from the side chair, saying nothing, but his ears were alert, begging for a report.

"Soon," Edward said. "He'll have an answer shortly. That's the quote."

Andreason leaned back in his chair and pulled out his pipe kit. Together they lit up and smoked in silence, reviewing the events of the past weeks. An hour passed. Then two. The stale air allowed the cloud of smoke to thicken.

Neither said a word.

"Well, gents," Superintendent McCarthy began, breaking the silence, then waved his hand to clear a hole in the smoke. Both policemen snapped to attention, cradling their pipes. "Seems like you have found a way to be alone with your thoughts. Nevertheless, Councilor Beechcroft has agreed to your request. You may serve the warrant tomorrow morning.

"This should cover every aspect of the bank," He handed Edward a sealed paper. "Break the seal in the morning, and take as many men with you as you need. Use my authority for the manpower."

"Thank you, sir," Edward said, and placed the document in his personal safe.

"You're welcome. Now, you and Officer Andreason get some sleep. You need to be sharp in the morning."

"Yes, sir." The two policemen reached for their coats and nodded on their way to the door. Edward felt much lighter.

16 February 1892, 0800:

"Ah, yes," Edward said, looking over a group of detectives. "Cadets Peterson and Brown, exactly on time. Are ye up for a visit to the Fisherman's Bank?"

"Yes, sir!" the two chorused.

"We are certain of our individual responsibilities?" The dozen plain-clothed officers all nodded. "Then let's go." The group turned and trotted to waiting carts and in seconds were rolling toward their destination. Peterson and Brown sat next to Officer Andreason in the lead wagon. Edward studied their shocked faces and smiled.

"We got the warrant last night, but there was little need to alert you," Edward began. "Officer Andreason and I decided it was better if you two got some much-needed sleep."

"Does this mean we're close to being finished?"

"On the contrary," one of the Scotland Yard Detectives interrupted. "Regularly, this means the case just became more entangled."

"Never let minor successes convince you to close a case too soon," said another.

"You two have done excellent work here," Edward said. "And these detectives are correct. A major milestone in any case rarely points to a conclusion. It may, on the contrary, make the case larger, it's end farther away. It could just as easily point to a quick end. We'll be at the bank in five minutes. Notebooks out. Write down how you would proceed inside the bank. Then note how it actually happens."

16 February 1892, 0955:

The wagons rocked and jostled toward their destination, one stopping at the front door to the bank. Another turned down the alley behind the building, and four officers set up watch to ensure no one left too early. Edward Willoughby and several officers cloistered about the entrance, while others took up guard stations up and down the street.

Peterson and Brown trotted past the snorting horses' steamy muzzles and jumped onto the walk. The veteran detectives pushed the young men toward the front of the line so they would enter just behind Andreason, who was behind Willoughby.

Identification wallet out, hand on the door, Edward Willoughby looked at his team of officers. He took a deep breath and pulled on the brass handle. The glass door opened and the line of men entered as a snake, sliding into the foyer of the facility as one. One man raced forward to greet the police.

"Peterson, is this the man?" Edward said.

"No sir, that one is," Peterson pointed to a distant desk.

A mouse of a man looked up at a finger directed his way. He looked left and right, but two detectives had already moved to block his path. He settled back into his chair, pushing himself away from his desk.

"Is that you, sir?" Edward said, walking toward the man. He pointed to the desk plate which said "Roger Whitehead".

The man nodded.

"What is the meaning of this interruption?" The first man said.

"Detective Edward Willoughby, Scotland Yard," Edward said, showing his identification. "And you would be?"

"Walter Brooks, branch manager of the Fisherman's Bank."

"Mister Brooks, I have a search warrant to inspect any and all records handled by Olivia Collingworth and Roger Whitehead, together or separately. This includes any safe deposit boxes, etcetera, with which they may be involved."

"If you could say what this is pertaining to," Walter said, "I might be of some help."

"This is an ongoing investigation, sir," Edward cleared his throat. "I am not at liberty to discuss the details. Mister Whitehead, you have had recent dealings with Mrs. Collingworth. Please, is there a place which would afford some privacy?"

"My office, Detective," Walter said, motioning to a heavy door at the rear of the bank. A pale Roger Whitehead followed the branch manager to the rear of the bank. Edward's team watched the employees, while a runner trotted outside and around to the rear to inform the rest of the team as to what was transpiring inside.

"I swear," Roger said, "I only helped her with a safe deposit box. I have no idea what is in it."

"What is the box number?" Edward said.

"The box number?" Roger said. "I would have to look at the log."

"No need." Walter produced a small notebook. "What time was the visit?"

"2:16 p.m. yesterday," Peterson said.

"Hmmpf. We'll see." Roger started to leave. Andreason blocked his path.

"You'll understand, sir," Robert said, "if we accompany you in this endeavor."

"What? Oh, of course. Sorry. This way." And off they went, Andreason and one of the other detectives, to the log sheet.

16 February 1892, 1022:

"Ah! Here it is." Walter looked up from the paper. "A Mrs. Longhorn was here, but not a Mrs. Collingworth."

"What did Mrs. Longhorn look like?" Andreason asked.

"A street person," a young woman nearby said. "She comes in every Friday, asks to see Mister Whitehead. They retreat to the safe deposit boxes."

"Irregular," Walter said. "Well, let's look at box 467, then."

The vault door was already open, with an armed guard sitting behind a desk near it. The procession neared the guard, who snapped to attention upon seeing Walter Brooks.

"The police and I are going to examine one of the boxes, Harold," Walter said.

"Very good, sir," and the guard sat back down.

The room was surrounded by silver-colored metal doors, all with numbers. Walter browsed through the rows and rows of the rectangles and stopped at a rather large one.

"Ah, here it is. 467." Walter said. He inserted two keys, pulled out the box and set it on the table in the middle of the room.

"Mister Brooks," Andreason said. "I think we can take it from here."

"Oh. Very good." Walter turned and left the vault.

Robert caught himself then looked at the other policemen. He took a deep breath, opened the lid, and stopped cold.

There were piles of money, neatly stacked, with a journal on top of it all. It would take a long time to count it and would require a team of accountants. Robert fingered the journal, fearing that if he opened it some serpent would attack him. Then with some hesitation, he flipped open to the first page.

"Penny Farthing, LLC. Journal beginning 1 July 1870." Andreason mumbled the words as he scanned the page then stopped at an entry near the top.

"This is blood money, gents" Andreason said. "The garment factory fires, to be exact. No one comes or goes." The two detectives nodded, and Robert trotted to the Branch Manager's office.

16 February 1892, 1240:

The door opened, and Robert Andreason poked his head inside. Edward looked up. Andreason smiled.

"A moment, gents," Edward excused himself. Once outside of the office, he asked "What did you find?"

"The holy grail," Robert said. "The money *and* the journal."

"Show me."

16 February 1892, 1247:

Edward stared at the money then flipped through the ledger entries. Years and years of entries, thousands or millions of pounds, and enough deceit to go around for everyone.

"They hid this well." Edward looked up at Andreason. "Looks like Mister Alexander has pointed us to another contractor for murder." Andreason pointed to a recent journal entry.

"See here?" Andreason held his finger on a column near the middle of the page. "Only one withdraw in years. To EFJA, a week ago. For 10,000 pounds."

"I believe Olivia could have paid a neighbor to do this for a lot less money."

"Perhaps. But that would be traceable. Someone would have talked, if only to brag about it."

"And Olivia did not want a failure," said one of the other detectives. "So she trusted the murder to a professional."

"Why did she even bother to write it down?" Robert scratched his head at this point.

"Everyone reports to someone," Edward replied. "It's possible John Collingworth became a liability, and whoever handles this money ordered his demise.

"Francis, Lawrence," Edward said to the two detectives, "due to the amount of money involved here, I am ordering an armed detachment to get this box to Scotland Yard. Stay here until they arrive." They nodded, and Edward tucked the journal under his arm as he and Andreason walked back to the branch manager's office.

Eight

Edward strode through the heavy Scotland Yard doors and up to Desk Sergeant Albert Johnson, who was busy making a log entry. His trimmed beard bounced as he wrote. Edward waited.

"She's in Interrogation Room Two, Edward," Albert said, not looking up from his entry. "And she is anything but happy to be here."

"Indeed." Edward smirked. "Thank you, Detective Sergeant Johnson."

"You're welcome." Albert continued to write.

Edward Willoughby, Patrolman Robert Andreason, Colin Peterson, and Emmitt Brown entered the small room together. The two cadets took chairs against the wall, while Edward and Robert sat at the table opposite Olivia Collingworth.

"Four coppers?" Olivia said. "You need four coppers to question me?"

"Actually, Missus Collingwood, you only have me." Edward eyed her demeanor. "The two young lads there are cadets. They are learning what it means to be a detective. Patrolman Andreason here is to keep me under control. Evidently you believe I pursue the wrong people for grievous crimes. Let's chat, shall we?"

"It's your time," she said.

"Tell me about Harold's Flowers."

"What about 'arold's Flowers? It's a shop two blocks from me 'ouse."

"Tell me about your Fridays."

"What I do on me Fridays is none o' your concern."

"We here at Scotland Yard determine what is of our concern. Now, answer the question."

"I go to 'arold's each Friday," Olivia appeared a shade paler, if that was even possible. "I pick up a parcel and drop it at a bank. I then go 'ome. That's all."

"What about Sunninghill?"

"You bastard!" She stood and screamed. "You *followed* me?"

"Answer the question." Edward leaned back in his chair and folded his hands in his lap. "What about Sunninghill?"

Cadets Brown and Peterson wrote furiously in their notebooks. Andreason's eyes flicked back forth, watching Olivia and Edward alternately. Olivia lowered her head, almost touching the table. When she raised up, her countenance had changed. A dark aura seemed to surround her.

"All I do is 'and a package to a man," she took several deep breaths. "He 'ands me a package."

"What's in the package you deliver?"

"I don't know."

"I doubt that."

"I know better than to ask." Olivia's hardened face seemed to reach across the table.

"You never opened the package?"

"It's sealed. If I opened it, I wouldn't live through the day."

"What's in the package you receive in Sunninghill?"

"I don't know."

"Where do you take it?"

"To the Fisherman's Bank."

"Who did you see there?"

"Just some man."

"Come, Come, Missus Collingworth." Edward leaned forward. "*Some* man doesn't help, and I doubt you would hand a surreptitious package to just anyone."

"Oh, all right. Roger Whitehead. 'e would take me to where the safe deposit boxes are, and I would just leave the package in the box 'e opened."

"What number?"

"468. They always left payment for me in the box. A 'undred quid."

"We'll check, of course. You're certain of the box number?"

"Of course. 468."

16 February 1892, 1900 Fisherman's Bank:

Two uniformed bobbies were standing watch over the safety deposit box room when Edward Willoughby, Patrolman Andreason, and Walter Brooks entered. They strode directly to box 468 and Walter Brooks inserted the keys. The branch manager retreated to the safety deposit box lounge while the Scotland Yard detective inspected its contents.

"Ready?" breathed Edward.

"No time like the present," Robert said.

Edward's fingers twisted the keys in the locks then opened the top. The box was empty, save for an envelope. He opened the flap and counted the notes. One hundred Pounds. Exactly.

"Tell me we still have Roger Whitehead in custody," Edward said.

"Yes," Robert said. "We're holding him for lying to us. Are you thinking he's the bookkeeper?"

"He certainly has the expertise. Mrs. Collingworth is merely a bag woman." Edward looked toward the door. "Mister Brooks?"

"Sir?" The banker poked his head inside.

"Who pays for box 468?"

"One moment, I'll check," He said.

"Officer Andreason will go with you." Edward nodded to Robert.

"Very good, sir."

"One more thing," Edward thought a moment, "bring the log back with you, if you please."

"Sir," Walter said, and he left with Andreason on his heals.

The two men left the room. Edward studied the safe deposit boxes, noting the position of the larger boxes. There was a pattern. He hoped he was wrong, but there were a lot of them.

Andreason and Brooks returned, and Edward searched his partner's eyes for a clue. Andreason's eyes had taken on a hard look, with a determination he had not seen before.

"Detective Willoughby," Walter Brooks began, "Box 486 belongs to Deborah Cornelius. It seems Officer Andreason recognizes the name."

"Deborah Cornelius is one of the deceased," Andreason said. "Adeline Longhorn is also one of the dead. We need the list from the Yard."

"Indeed," Edward said. He looked out the door. "Peterson! Brown!"

"Yessir," the two cadets poked their heads inside the room.

"You know where the list of the dead from the garment factory fires is located on my desk?" Edward retrieved his keys from his pocket.

"Yes, sir," Peterson said. "But if you need it, we need not retrieve it. I kept a copy of the list in my coat pocket, to remind me who we are trying to get justice for." He reached inside his coat and handed a folded piece of paper to Edward, who received the document with trembling hands.

"Good lad!" cried Robert Andreason

"Detective Willoughby has his hat," said Cadet Peterson. "I have this."

"And we shan't keep it from you long." Edward spread the paper on the table in the middle of the room, then opened the ledger for the safety deposit boxes. "Sharp eyes, gents. Colin and Emmitt will monitor the list of the deceased, and Robert and I will read the names of the owners of the boxes."

16 February 1892, 2300:

An hour passed, and Edward closed and pushed the ledger away from him. Twenty-three safe deposit boxes were open, all full of currency, and each with their own ledger. He turned slowly and surveyed the scene before him, his eyes resting on Walter Brooks, who cleaned his spectacles for the hundredth time.

"How is this possible?" Walter's pleading eyes looked up at Detective Willoughby.

"We *will* find out, sir. That is a promise we all owe to those poor souls who perished." Edward sighed, looking into one of the boxes. "It looks like these are all ten pound notes. Give me an educated guess as to the value of this one box."

"That may be impossible…no, wait!" Walter turned to the door. "Catherine!"

"Yes, sir?"

"Bring me a bundle of ten pound notes, please."

"Yes, sir." The young woman appeared a moment with one bundle of bills in her hand.

"Thank you Catherine. Also, please bring me my Thatcher scale."

"Yes, sir."

Walter produced a small ruler, and measured the bills. "One Inch and three quarters. Will you assist me detective?"

"Certainly."

"Press down hard on this first stack, as though it were bundled." Walter took a deep breath. "Yes, just like that."

Walter inserted the ruler inside the box and carefully measured the stack.

"Ten inches and one quarter." Walter looked behind him, and Catherine handed him a bamboo cylinder, with lateral slides and scales of varying kinds on it. He set the device on the table, and moved the slides to specific points. "Divided by one point…each stack is worth 5,857 pounds sterling. Twelve stacks to a box…"he checked his arithmetic twice. "It's only an estimate, though." He wrote the number: £1,616,571.

"This will get some attention," Lawrence whistled.

"Indeed," Edward said. "Be a good lad, and order another armed detail to get this to Scotland Yard. And do keep this quiet."

"Sir." The Detective saluted and trotted out the door.

"Robert, you and I have an appointment at Kentish Station, with Roger Whitehead." Edward rubbed his tired eyes.

"Yes, sir, we do." Robert scratched his mustache on the right side. "Now or in the morning?"

"Now. Before the jailer forgets why he is in custody."

Nine

Roger Whitehead fidgeted. He was only being detained because he was not forthcoming with the truth about the safe deposit boxes. *That's all it could be, isn't it?* He thought furiously. *They couldn't know, could they? I was so careful.*

The holding cell at Kentish Station was a small affair, not designed to hold many people. Today it was half full of a range of people being detained. The floor was cleaned twice a day, due to what drunks would leave there, though the cleaning never quite got rid of the smell. Roger held a white kerchief to his nose.

The door with the bars on it opened. The copper looked straight at Roger. *Good. I am being released.*

"Roger Whitehead," the policeman said.

"Yes," Roger answered.

"Come with me."

"Being released, eh?"

"Evidently the detective in charge has some more questions."

Roger's heart sank. His knees became weak, and he almost collapsed. The Bobbie kept him from hitting the floor.

"Steady, laddie," the policeman said. "It's off to Interrogation Room Three."

Roger was half-walked, half-dragged down the long hallway.

17 February 1892, 0120:

"How did our boy do?" Edward asked the Bobbie.

"Not so good," the policeman said, with a smirk. "When 'e found out 'e was to go to interrogation, 'e nearly collapsed."

"Thank you. I believe we'll have a go at Mister Whitehead." Edward stroked his chin. "Officer Andreason, care to assist?"

"Wouldn't miss it." Robert had a gleam in his eyes. They entered the hallway and walked toward the interrogation room.

17 February 1892, 0130:

Roger Whitehead studied his manacles briefly, then lay his head on the table. The small room was a plain gray color, devoid of windows or trappings. Just one table and three chairs.

The door opened. Edward Willoughby and Officer Andreason entered. Edward carried a sheaf of papers in one hand and a cup of tea in the other. Officer Andreason carried nothing, save his stern look.

"Ah, Mister Whitehead," Edward gave him a quick glance.

"I'm certain you're aware it's 1:30 in the morning. Let's get on with it. Ask your questions."

"Very well," Edward and Robert sat on chairs opposite the banker. "We have found some irregularities in the safe deposit room of The Fisherman's Bank."

"What sort of irregularities?" Roger's expression did not change.

"Several of the boxes belong to dead people."

"Dead people? How is that possible?"

"The problem here is Officer Andreason has a near-perfect memory."

"Oh?"

"When we began looking at the owners of the boxes, he began to notice a pattern. Specifically, they belong to women who died in the Garment Factory Fires seven years past."

"Oh, I remember that fire. Ghastly stuff, that."

"Indeed." Edward cleared his throat. "There's more."

"More?" Roger shrank in his chair.

"All the boxes are full of British Sterling Notes."

"Ten pound notes you say?"

"Actually, I didn't say." Edward watched Roger become ashen. "The totals are astronomical. We only opened twenty-three boxes and then did a quick estimate at 1,600,000 pounds. It is only an estimate, you see."

"Yes, I see. It would take a very long time to actually count that many ten pound notes."

"There was only one withdraw in the past ten years. £10,000 given to EFJA. It also seems the person paying for all the boxes is— would you care to guess, sir?"

"You act as if you already know."

"Excellent deduction." Another sip of tea. "The boxes are all paid for by a Roger Whitehead. That would be you, sir. Or is it a monumental coincidence?"

"Why deny it?"

"Why indeed?" Another sip of tea. "You're saying you admit it?"

Roger looked up at Edward. His eyes were pleading with the detective. "Promise me you'll protect my family."

"If they are involved with this, I cannot."

"They are not involved." Roger wiped his brow with his handkerchief. "I swear by all that is holy they are not. EFJA, you say? I'm not certain who that is."

"Come, come now," Edward leaned back in his chair. "You mean to have me believe you gave 10,000 pounds sterling to a complete stranger?"

"Not in the least. What I am saying is I never met Mister Alexander."

"Who's Mister Alexander?" Robert said.

"Didn't you just say that name?"

"No, we did not," Edward glared.

"Sure you…"

"We only identified a set of letters, nothing else." Edward leaned forward. "Answer the question. Who is Mister Alexander?"

"Please," Roger looked longingly at the door. "I can't."

"Why not?"

"I just can't."

"Well, then," Edward looked at a different document from a different folder. "We can neatly tie a murder charge around your neck."

"Murder?" Roger stood. "Murder!"

"Sit down, Mister Whitehead." Andreason stood, his fists at the ready.

"Oh, dear god," Roger sat and placed his head in his hands. "What have I gotten myself into?"

"A pile of trouble, Mister Whitehead." Edward continued to stare at the banker. "Larger than any you can possibly imagine." He slid a piece of paper across the table. "Now, write it down."

"I can give you everything," Roger sobbed. "Everything except Mister Alexander. He'll kill my family. There is naught you can do to protect them."

"Give us what you can," Edward said. "We'll let you know if it is enough."

Roger began writing and did not stop for several hours. He detailed the money drops, the safe deposit boxes, what came out of the florist shop, and to whom it was directed. There were individuals shrouded in foggy nights and shadows, but others used go-betweens, or drop locations. It was 30 years of corruption and graft.

Nothing on E.F.J. Alexander.

17 February 1892, 0330:

Roger pushed himself back from the table. "That's it," he sighed. "That's all I can give you."

"What about Mister Alexander?" Edward said.

"I already said," Roger eyed the detective, "my family will be forfeit."

"I sincerely hope you will reconsider," Edward finished his fourth cup of tea. "We have a whole empire in which to hide you and your family."

"We'll never make it to trial!" He looked back and forth at both policemen. "Don't you see the position I'm in?"

"Not much different from the position of the 294 women who perished in the garment factory fires." Edward sighed. "We're going to need one more item from you."

"Haven't I given you enough? What more could you possibly ask of me?"

"Nothing. Absolutely nothing." Edward looked at Robert.

"We want you to act absolutely normal for the next week," Robert Andreason said. "Tell everyone you know this has all been a misunderstanding."

"What?"

"This coming Friday will be your last at the bank. You help us with this, and I personally promise you leniency."

Ten

Olivia Collingworth left her flat at precisely eleven, as was her custom. She browsed the usual street vendors, offering the same arguments to the same proprietors she always did.

Harold's Florist Shoppe was still in the same condition it always was. A gentleman wearing a bowler hat and a tweed suit browsed tulips in one corner. A man pondered roses. Olivia entered as she always did.

"Mister James," Olivia began, "it's such a lovely day outside. You should get out and see it."

"I will indeed, Mrs. Longhorn," the proprietor used the name on the safe deposit box and walked to the counter in the rear of the shop. "I have your order of fertilizer right here." He pulled out a heavily wrapped package and handed it to her.

"Thank you, Mister James," Olivia said. "See you next week."

"Good day, Mrs. Longhorn."

Olivia walked outside to the curb and hailed a cab. Charlie the cabbie pulled up and whisked her away to her second destination. Edward Willoughby and Robert Andreason were in the rear. They had rigged a privacy curtain, concealing their position in the cab.

The driver made his way through the working class neighborhoods, to better environs, finishing among the homes of the well-to-do. He stopped at the same address in Sunninghill as Cadet Peterson had written down a few days before.

The footman opened the low gate facing the street. He was well-dressed man who could be attending a formal function. The middle-aged man looked up and down the street, pulled a packet from inside his coat, and handed it to Olivia. She took the packet and handed the package from the Florist to him. No words were exchanged.

"Excuse me, kind sir," Edward addressed the footman as he placed his hand on the gate to re-enter the residence. "Would you perhaps know the way to Scotland Yard?"

"That would be in Kensington…" he looked about him, noting a half dozen determined men surrounding him. "I think you already know where Scotland Yard is."

"Indeed," Edward said and held his identification. "Edward Willoughby, detective, Scotland Yard. I have a search warrant for the property before you and any other you planned on entering."

"Who says I planned on entering any other property?"

"I do," Cadet Peterson said. "You will enter the outbuilding on the right and emerge within 15 minutes. You will at that time return to the main house. My assumption is to return to your 'regular' assignment."

"Lying to us will not help your situation," Edward said. "We will follow as you make your delivery."

"And what makes you think I will make the delivery?" the footman said.

"I will change the charges to multiple murders and let the justice system sort you out. You do know the penalty for murder?"

"I've killed no one."

"You've abetted in the murder of 294 women." Edward studied the man's reaction. "As such, you are guilty by association. Do not trifle with me, sir. This is not my first circus."

"How many?" The footman's jaw had dropped open.

"294. Now move."

22 February 1892, 1200:

Key in the door. One full turn to the right. The footman stepped inside the building. Edward led the Scotland Yard detectives as they spread out in what was obviously a laboratory. Numerous glass flasks, tubes, and bottles of powders of varying colors lined the tables. It all appeared as chaos.

"Place it on the table and get out." A balding man peered through a magnifying glass without looking up.

"I'm afraid there will be a change in your routine today, sir." Edward looked at the man, whose large apron covered him from ankle to chest. "Please step away from your work."

"I'm unaccustomed to being interrupted," the man sneered. "Do you know who I am?"

"Doctor Neville Garner," Edward responded.

"Ah, Detective Willoughby," Neville said. "Then you know I have friends in high places."

"Higher than Queen Victoria?"

"Oh," Neville said. "You are one of those pedants constantly throwing royalty names about then?"

"Almost never," Edward said. "But we were about to enter a debate, which I wanted to stifle quickly. Considering the layout of your laboratory, I assume the package contains opium."

"You have proof?"

"Not yet but I've seen opium laboratories before." Edward scanned the room. "Yours is not unique."

"There's where you would be wrong, Detective." Neville looked at the hardened faces in the room. "My purity is beyond question, demanding the highest price."

"I'll take that as an admission of guilt, sir." Edward looked at the package on the table. "I don't see a customs stamp on the package. Now we are looking at smuggling, on top of everything else."

"Everything else?"

"Unlawful imprisonment, slavery, and murder for starters."

"What?"

"You heard me. And that's just for starters."

"You have no proof!"

"You have no idea what I have." Edward looked about the room, noting the cleanliness of it all. "By the time I am done with you, your bloody hand will reach from here to China and back again. Sir, step away from the table and place your hands behind you. Officer Andreason, if you would be so kind."

"With pleasure," Robert said. "Sir, your hands please."

"I have a batch in progress," Neville said. "Stop now and it will be ruined."

Edward walked to the worktable and turned the gas to the burner off. "That it will be ruined is not my problem."

"You have no concept of the magnitude of this business, do you?" Neville glared at the detective, as Officer Andreason placed the manacles about his wrists.

"I have a perfect concept of this 'business', as you call it." Edward's face was just inches from Neville's. "I see it every day of my life, in ruined lives and castaways on the streets. I see families torn apart by the vile serum you peddle as something 'helpful'. You are the worst scum, because you look down from your ivory tower and believe you are above the law.

"Let me inform you, sir, you are not. The longer you reside in prison, the better."

'This way, sir.' Robert led Neville Garner out to a waiting paddy wagon.

"Okay, lads," Edward began, "we want to avoid the chemicals. We are now looking for any and all documentation of this trade. In any language, including Oriental. We can translate everything later. Lawrence, Franklin, would you be so kind as to accompany me into the main house?"

22 February 1892, 1230:

Edward twisted the doorbell as two detectives stood behind him. At the third ring, an elegant woman opened the door.

"I apologize, sir. I can't seem to find my footman at the moment." The woman in her mid-forties pushed back a loose strand of hair. "How may I help you?"

"I'm Detective Edward Willoughby of Scotland Yard, and these two gentlemen are my associates."

"Scotland Yard?" the woman said. "What's amiss?"

"We have a warrant to search the premises. And your footman is safe but in our custody, hence his absence. You are Louisiana Garner?"

"I am."

"The warrant does not include you, madam, but we are required to search your residence."

"What is it you seek?"

"Any and all information as to your husband's business dealings." Edward handed her a document. "You may wish to read the warrant."

"My husband is retired." Louisiana said. "His only business dealings are with the bank."

"We shall soon find out. Please step aside."

"Not until my husband confers with me."

"I'm afraid he, too, is in our custody; so that will not be possible at the moment."

"Then I must protest."

"Protest you may, but the warrant is for an immediate search." Edward pushed past the startled woman. The number of detectives on the porch now totaled a dozen, and all of them streamed into the estate.

"There's no need to be brutish," Louisiana said.

"We are not in the practice of being delayed in the execution of a warrant, be it intentional or not." Edward's face softened.

"I realize this is a troubling event, but the more you cooperate, the sooner it will be over." Edward waved his hand to the parlor. "Please sit. Do you have any other servants in the house?"

"Only Clara, my cook."

"Where?"

"In the basement."

"Franklin?" Edward said.

"On it," Franklin walked to the stairs.

"Where is your husband's study?" Edward studied the beautiful woman's face.

"In there," she pointed.

"Got it," Lawrence said, striding toward the ornate entrance.

Franklin returned with a shocked woman in cook's attire. "Please sit here until our search is complete." Franklin looked at Edward. "I have this. I think Lawrence could use some assistance."

Edward arrived in the room. *Study...doesn't quite cover it,* thought Edward, *this is a full library with a desk.* He scanned everything. The well-stocked room would be any book-lover's dream. Lawrence was struggling with the desk drawers. Edward stepped back into the parlor.

"Mrs. Garner, do you have the keys to your husband's desk?"

"No, Detective, he keeps those with him."

"Thank you," Edward said. "Lawrence, I will be back shortly."

Edward strode to the paddy wagon. The Sergeant snapped to attention.

"Sergeant," Edward began, "when we searched Mr. Garner, was he in possession of keys?"

"Yessir, 'e was. Just a minute." He turned and retrieved a bag from the locked compartment of the wagon. "Ah, yes, keys. 'ere you go, Detective."

"Thank you. I'll return them as soon as our search is complete."

"Detective?" The Bobbie asked.

"Yes, sergeant?"

"What 'as Mr. Garner done?"

"I'm not at liberty to say, but you can be certain he committed at least one felony."

"Thank you, sir."

Eleven

22 February 1892, 1730:

"We counted the contents of the package delivered to the Fisherman's Bank," Cadet Brown began. "It contained 1,500 pounds worth of ten pound notes. Exactly."

"Multiply that by 52," Cadet Peterson added, "equals 78,000 pounds per year, for just one of the safe deposit boxes. If all the safe deposit boxes contain the same amount, then the total is 1,794,000 pounds. The banker's estimate was not far off the mark."

"Indeed," Edward said, leaning back in his chair at Scotland Yard. "Yet I believe Mister Garner is not the head of any organization. He is merely a worker in a long chain of workers. The fact that he already has money makes this little more than a pastime for him."

"We follow the money," Andreason said. "The footman began talking an hour ago and showed us where the money came from. We begin pursuing that lead tomorrow.

"The florist, on the other hand," Edward said, "is as tight as a clam. The same magistrate will prosecute him to the maximum extent of the law if he does hot help us. The initial sentence is 15 years. He does not know it, but we found his ledgers beneath his orchid collection.

"Our accountants are reviewing all the books, but we need to proceed before anyone knows we have detained anyone."

"What about Olivia Collingworth?" Cadet Brown asked.

"I have already spoken with the local magistrate," Edward said. "He said if she fully cooperates, he will commute her sentence. Her crime is minor and her situation could turn dire if arrested. Placing her in prison will serve no purpose.

"I would hope she saved her courier money. Robbie Collingworth displays the potential to make something of himself. Olivia seems bent on a proper education for her children, and perhaps London might be better for it."

23 February 1892, 0800:

Harold's Florist Shop opened promptly at 8:00 o'clock the following morning, staffed by two Scotland Yard Detectives. Customers flowed in and out of the shop, and as things slowed in the afternoon, an oriental gentleman wearing a suit, a frock coat, and a derby hat stepped to the counter.

"Where's Mister Sands?" he asked the detective at the counter. "Off sick. Has a terrible cough."

"And you are?" The man twirled his thin mustache. He appeared about 30 years old, and his hands showed the calluses and scars of a brawler.

"Franklin McTavish. Martin Sand's cousin from Stoke. Just arrived on this morning's train. You might be?"

"I have some personal business with Mister Sands." His dark eyes looked all the way around the shop, coming to rest on the man behind the counter.

"Martin said I could conduct all business of the shop in his name."

"Not this." The man turned to leave, when Lawrence held his badge and blocked his path.

"This is a butterfly knife," the man said, producing a long, thin blade. "Whores in Hong Kong use this weapon to cut the testicles off men who assault them. Step aside, and we'll have no problem."

"This is the business end of a .577 Webley," Franklin said, pulling a revolver from his coat pocket. "It's so powerful, it's liable to cut you clean in half. Drop the knife, and we'll have a lovely chat."

The man looked over his shoulder at Franklin then back at the Lawrence standing in the doorway. He smiled and dropped the knife, point first, into the plank floor. Edward Willoughby and Officer Andreason walked through the door.

"On your knees," Edward said. The man complied. "Good. Now, cross your legs. Franklin, you have him covered?"

"I got the bugger all right." Franklin grinned.

"Lawrence," Edward said, "Manacle the gentleman."

Lawrence walked around the man, careful to keep from Franklin's line of fire. The manacles installed, Lawrence hauled him to his feet. He patted the man down and removed a package similar to the one containing the opium delivered to Dr. Garner. Lawrence pulled several small trinkets from the man's pockets and dropped them into a bag held by Edward.

Four detectives escorted the suspect to a waiting paddy wagon. The wagon was barely out of sight when Edward spread the contents of the bag on the counter of the shop. Three six-sided dice, a calling card with an address in Wandsworth, and a scrap of paper with £333 written on it. Edward spread the paper out and studied it.

"Not your normal paper, Robert," Edward said. "Very thick. Origin is Eastern, possibly Egyptian or Chinese. The single item is curious: £333."

"Nothing domestic, either," Robert said. "No house key, no money, nothing to trade for even a pint at a pub."

"I wonder if the dice are designed to do that at some club," Edward scratched his chin. "Perhaps the note is his line of credit?"

"That would buy a lot," Robert said. "I've never seen a club or pub manage indebtedness this way. Ps and Qs, yes, but not by way of a note. I could imagine several of the opium dens near the waterfront doing this, though."

"May I?" Cadet Brown reached for the die and the stones. "Arrange them like so. What do you see?"

"333," Edward said. "A password?"

"To a special place, possibly a club," the cadet said. "Hold them in your hand, arranged properly, and you gain admittance."

"I believe we might find the answer in Wandsworth." Edward mused, hands folded behind him.

"Indeed," Cadet Brown said. He smiled and mimicked the posture of Edward.

Twelve

Crumpled newspapers tumbled down the block as the intense wind attempted to clean the streets of anything not held in place. Fog and snow billowed around the corners of the brick buildings, and the few people out of doors did their best to get inside, out of the cold.

Edward observed a line of people waiting to enter an establishment with "Частный клуб" for a nameplate, with a police baton mounted next to it. These were well-dressed individuals, who did their best to brace against the cold, though not successfully. They all waited patiently to gain entrance.

The two policemen took their place at the end of the line and waited with everyone else. A dozen detectives watched from behind a glass door just down the street.

No one spoke.

They observed the gentleman in front of them arrange his dice to make 636; so he arranged his own to do the same. The guard at the door looked at each man's hands and then granted admission.

Edward's turn. He showed his hand to the guard.

"What do you take me for, a fool?" the large man sneered. "Get out of here! Now!"

"Wait," Edward said. He displayed his badge and said "will this do instead?"

The guard turned to retreat inside the building when Willoughby and Andreason grabbed him, turned him around, and cuffed his hands. The detectives poured out of their observation position and ran up the street.

"Run, will you?" Andreason said, grunting as the two policemen held the man against the wall. "I don't like it when buggers like you run. Makes me suspicious of your intentions."

"I have him Robert," Franklin said, taking over for Andreason. "Go. Serve your warrant." He turned to the guard. "You. When a copper shows 'is badge, the *last* thing you do is run."

Edward and Robert opened the heavy steel door, and a dozen detectives entered the building. They were greeted by opulence everywhere. Velvet drapes and oak paneling covered the walls. Oriental fabric covered the sofas and chairs, which were occupied by beautiful Asian women.

Well-heeled gentlemen were in various forms of conversation with women and other men. A gigantic bar lined the side of the lobby. Tobacco smoke filled the air, and hostesses with drinks circulated throughout the room. Several billiard tables could be seen in the distance, most of which were in use.

"What can Častnyj klub do for Scotland Yard today?" A stunning occidental woman asked in a Slavic accent. She was a heart-stopper, and her white flowing dress illuminated her in the dim light. Her hair was an artistic and ornamental style with a beautiful woven pattern adorned on top by a black ribbon. Pearls were in a woven pattern in the rear, and her black hair flowed on to her shoulders. She wore little make up, save bright red lip rouge, and her smile melted the hardened attitude of the detectives. "I'm Valeriya Tatyana Kipriyanov. You may call me Valeriya, or Valerie, whichever is easier."

"Detective Edward Willoughby. Are you the proprietor of this establishment?"

"I am owner and proprietor of Častnyj klub, and I know what you are about to say. I am allowed to own real estate property in England because my heritage did not begin in this country, but in Russia."

"I'm not concerned regarding your standing as a land owner, Valeriya, but we are looking for one particular individual we took into custody yesterday. He was well-dressed, but his pockets contained a minimal amount of items."

"Such as?"

"Three dice, a card for this establishment, and a note with one 333 written on it." Edward paused, let the items register with Valeriya. "Do any or all of these ring a bell?"

"Why yes, they do," Valeriya said. "They belong to an unsavory gent named Tom Whang. He keeps a locker here with personal items in it. If you have a warrant, I will be happy to open it for you."

"We do," Edward said, presenting Valeriya with the document. "Later, could you explain the code of the dice?"

"I'd be delighted, detective." She scanned the warrant, then handed it back to Edward. "Right this way."

Edward Willoughby and Robert Andreason followed Valeriya through the club, while the rest of the detectives waited at the front entrance. Another dozen detectives were positioned outside so that every door and window was covered.

Edward noted an ornate, carpeted stairway to the right, with a steady stream of patrons and employees ascending and descending the steps. The bar was relatively full, considering it was mid-morning, and some men were eating bangers and mash while drinking whiskey.

Valeriya socialized her way across the floor to the billiard room. She knew everyone by first name, and each man believed he was her best friend. All billiard play stopped as the trio entered, and Edward and Robert were now facing a hostile gathering of gentlemen.

"Pay them no mind, gents," Valeriya said. "These good people from Scotland Yard are in the process of removing Tommy Whang from our membership." She flirtaciously looked over her shoulder at Edward. "We have a strict policy regarding members being on the wrong side of the law."

They walked through to a locker room with several hundred boxes.

"Ah, here it is," Valeriya said. "Tom was very specific. It had to be box 333." She slipped the master key into the lock. Edward touched her arm.

"Please, madam," Edward said. "Let us take it from here."

"As you wish," her eyes twinkled. "And for what it's worth, I am not married. Madam would be an incorrect address."

"My apology," Edward tipped his hat. "Miss Kipriyanov."

"Thank you," she winked and walked a few paces toward the billiard room. "I will wait right here in case you need anything."

"Thank you." Edward twisted the key in the lock and opened the door. The locker was empty. He picked up an envelope in the bottom of the locker. A typewriter had written the following on the flap:

Detective Edward Willoughby

He opened the envelope, which contained a card and a single type-written sentence on a card:

The answers lie in Sunninghill.

"He is impressive, is he not?" Robert Andreason read the note over Edward's shoulder.

"Yes, he is," Edward said, then paused. "What did we miss in Sunninghill?"

"Obviously we need to return. We missed nothing in the house."

"What about the laboratory?"

Both policemen looked at each other and smiled.

"We still have it secured," Robert said.

"And there is much of the day left," Edward said. "Let's get the fresh eyes of our cadets involved."

"They would relish the opportunity."

Edward closed and locked the cabinet and walked to Valeriya. He handed her the key, and as she took it she wrapped her warm, soft fingers about Edwards' hand.

"Thank you, Miss Kipriyanov," Edward said, his heart beating faster than he wished. "I appreciate your assistance in this matter."

"You are welcome, Detective Willoughby." She paused, and then added, "May I call you Edward?"

"You may," Edward said, blushing ever so slightly.

"Then you may return to Častnyj klub any time you wish," she said.

"Pardon my ignorance, but what is the English translation for the Russian name of your establishment?"

"Private Club." Valeriya smiled again. "It is not complicated, but it does add a bit of mystery, having a Russian name."

"It does. I may take you up on your offer to return."

"In that case, here are your membership credentials," Valeriya handed Edward an envelope. "I am anticipating your return."

"Thank you once again, Miss Kipriyanov." Edward took the envelope, tipped his hat, and walked briskly to the front door.

Thirteen

23 February 1892, 1300:

As the caravan of wagons approached Sunninghill, Edward tucked the envelope in his coat pocket. He rubbed his hands and closed his eyes, creating a search plan for the laboratory.

"You should take Miss Kipriayanov up on her offer," Robert said. "I overheard two gents say how long it took to gain a membership at the club. You should feel privileged."

"I believe I shall, once this investigation is over," Edward never opened his envelope. "Do you think there might be something under the floor in the laboratory?"

"I'm up for anything," Robert answered.

23 February 1892, 1330:

Two bobbies stood guard at the door to the laboratory as Edward and the team of detectives entered the dark room. Nothing seemed to be disturbed, and they half expected to see Doctor Neville Garner working at his station.

Edward strode to the door and spoke to the bobbies.

"Has the Scotland Yard team been here yet?" Edward asked.

"Not yet, sir," one of them responded.

"Thank you."

Edward retreated back inside and slowly looked around the room, pausing on each bottle, every reagent, each odd plant. *It's not in plain sight,* Edward thought.

"The answer will not be obvious, gents," Edward said. "We need to look for hidden compartments, false walls, and trap doors."

"Hullo," Cadet Peterson said, his foot pointing at a worn spot by the main workbench. "It seems this table has been moved. And often."

A half dozen pairs of eyes stared at the floor. Andreason and Edward crouched and felt the marks.

"A bit deep, eh?" Robert said. "He's been moving this table for quite some time."

"Yes, quite," Edward said. "All right, let's see how one man could move such a heavy table."

"There!" Cadet Brown said, almost shouting. He pointed to a block and tackle on the far wall. He walked to the device, pulled its hook to the bench and slipped it onto a metal loop at the end of the tabletop. He then pulled the rope on the block to take up the strain. Once the rope was taut, he pulled hard and the table slid easily across the wood floor.

The trap door was now in plain view.

"The bugger lied to us," Lawrence said. He breathed through his teeth, and the veins on his temples stood out, pulsing rapidly. "I hate it when they do that."

"I brought four torches," Franklin said. Everyone stared at him. "Wot? It's dark in here." He set four kerosene bulls eye devices on the table, produced a box of matches, and proceeded to light all of them. "I just hope we're not entering the world of the macabre."

Edward pulled on the iron ring on the trap door, and it opened with a whoosh. A ladder pointed the way down. The musty smell flooded the room, and Andreason locked eyes with Willoughby.

"I've smelled this before, sir," Robert said.

"Likewise," Edward said, grasping one of the torches from the table. "Shall we?" and he took a step down the ladder.

The shaft was about four by four feet. Edward counted 21 steps to the bottom. He stepped onto a wood plank floor and illuminated as much as he could.

"A lateral shaft points toward the main house," Edward said.

"I'll come give you a hand," Robert said.

"Very well," Edward said. "Let's keep it to four people right now. One stays at the bottom of the ladder as a messenger."

"I'll be the messenger," Peterson said.

"Very good," Edward said. "Officer Andreason, it will be you and Franklin accompanying me in the shaft then."

The two policemen descended as Edward made his way through the lateral shaft. It was dirt reinforced by heavy timbers and was roughly seven feet tall. Periodically the men had to duck for the timbers, and within a hundred feet the shaft entered a large room.

Fourteen

Many eyes looked out of the darkness. Dozens of cages lined the huge room. Edward shined his light into the nearest prison. The face looking back at him was thin and pitiful.

"Do you have a name?" Edward asked.

"R-Ramona," came a hoarse whisper.

"Ramona, we are going to get all of you out of here," Edward tried to look as pleasant as possible.

"How does someone do this?" Andreason said.

"We're going to find out," Franklin said, tightening his fists.

"Over here, gents," Edward was pointing to the far wall. A door. He flipped a wall switch. The room was bathed in dim orange lighting, revealing the extent of the underground prison.

The cages were positioned like shelves in a library. They were three feet by three feet by six feet long. The occupants could not stand up, could barely stretch out, and had nowhere to relieve themselves. The smell was noxious.

"How do we get them out?" Franklin looked at the imposing door. "There's no way to take them up through the shaft."

"With this, I believe," Edward took a key from a hook on the wall. He inserted it into the keyhole and twisted it. Click! The deadbolt slid aside, and he turned the knob. Light spilled into the room as the door opened, and the three policemen looked into the basement of the Garner residence.

"Franklin," Edward thought fast, "ensure no one enters this room, save medical personnel. Robert, start on the right side. I'll begin on the left. We need a count of all souls in this room. And a medical facility large enough to take them all in."

Robert and Edward hurried from cage to cage, counting each body – dead or alive – and returned to the center of the room.

"Fifty one," Robert said.

"Fifty six," Edward added. "One hundred and seven. I will confer with Cadet Peterson and have the team re-enter the Garner residence." He ran down the shaft.

"Detective Willoughby," Peterson said.

"Cadet Peterson. Can you read this note?"

He scanned it, then looked up at Edward Willoughby. "You can't be serious?"

"Absolutely. Several are near death."

"Consider it delivered." Peterson scrambled up the vertical shaft to the laboratory. "Lawrence!"

"Yes?" Willoughby heard in the distance. Lawrence's face peered down the shaft, the note in his hand. "Edward, I understand. I have runners off to wire Scotland Yard for immediate assistance. We'll meet you in the basement."

"Very good." Edward tipped his hat and turned back to the underground prison.

Fifteen

A dozen ambulances raced to the Sunninghill residence, with others being dispatched from hospitals farther out. Each ambulance carried two orderlies and one doctor. The first team ran down the basement stairs with two stretchers.

"Dear lord in heaven," said the doctor as he stepped into the room. "Doctor William Wainsford. How may I be of service?"

"Doctor Wainsford," Edward said, "You need to focus your energies. Make brutal calls. Can you do that?"

"Sir, I am a trauma surgeon. I am trained for just this type of event. What do you want?"

"Take this chalk and mark the cages with the most critical cases with a 'C'. Mark the mortal cages with an 'M'. Evacuate the critical, non-critical and mortal cases, in that order."

"I understand. Brutal. But I understand."

"It's reality. It's what we had to do during the garment factory fires." A grim Edward Willoughby handed the doctor the chalk. "You do what you do well and I'll get them out of this hell."

"Right. Laddies, with me." The doctor strode to the first cage and marked it 'M'. The next with a 'C'. Franklin unlocked that cage and the orderlies gently lifted a frail woman onto the first stretcher. More teams arrived. Doctor Wainsford looked at the arriving doctors.

"Johnnie, this cage. Harry, this one. Morris, this one..." All the white-clad medical personnel leaped to their responsibilities.

Edward glanced at Lawrence at the top of the stairs. "Lawrence, make certain the critical cases go to the nearest hospitals."

"Right," Lawrence said. "The only choice is Saint Thomas."

"The most critical to the Kentish dispensary," Doctor Wainsford shouted. "Limit of twelve. The rest to Saint Thomas."

"You heard the man," Lawrence said to two stretcher-bearers, "are these *most* critical?"

"No sir," the orderly said. "There are several in worse state than these."

"Then it's off to Saint Thomas with you." Lawrence looked at Edward and said "I have this. Go. Save as many as you can."

Edward ran back into the prison to see the medical staff hard at work, a dozen stretchers holding patients. The doctors were shouting instructions back and forth to each other, orderlies grabbing patients and running to the exit, and one team still marking cages. He spotted Doctor Wainsford mark 'M' on a cage with a young child inside.

"No…" Edward said.

"Detective," Doctor Wainsford said, "she won't make it to Kentish dispensary, let alone Saint Thomas Hospital."

"Then I'll treat her here. What does she need?"

"Water. If she'll drink." Wainsford's sad eyes locked with Edward's. "I doubt she will."

"Robert. Water. Doctor, I will not let the youngest die without a fight."

"Very well," the doctor turned away then said, "I'll be back to lend a hand."

Edward reached into the cage and cradled the weak girl in his arms and walked to the central table. Tiny fingers reached for Edward's neck but fell away.

"Franklin, do the honors please."

Franklin swept the surface clean with one swipe of his huge arm, all items crashing into an unused corner. He then helped lower the girl onto the wood. A folded sheet landed nearby, an orderly nodded, then returned to his tasks.

Edward started to rest the girl's emaciated head onto the sheet, when delicate hands placed a satin pillow in place of the cotton fabric. Louisiana Garner began to drip water onto the parched lips from a soaked cloth, and a calloused tongue lapped up the life liquid.

"Would you arrest me, Detective Willoughby, if I killed my husband?" Louisiana dipped a cloth into the water and let the girl suck on it. "There, there, young lady. Not too much.

"I was a charge nurse in Crimea," she said. "Some of that was a bad as this. Bad, in a different way." She opened each of the young eyes and shined the lamp into them. "She *will* survive, Detective. I'll have it no other way. Don't you have someone to arrest?"

"I do, but I need to stay here." Edward and Franklin looked at each other. "Detective Sergeant Johnson."

"Lawrence," Edward shouted from the bottom of the stairs.

"Sir." Lawrence strained over the rail, listening over the din of the rescue in progress.

"Make haste and get word to Detective Sergeant Johnson," Edward was almost out of breath. "Neville Garner is to be arrested for murder and false imprisonment. Do not let that cretin out of Scotland Yard."

Sixteen

23 February 1892, 1530:

Edward rushed back to the table, where Louisiana continued to administer water to the young girl. The lady's hands were tender, her method deliberate.

"If you managed to kill your husband, m'lady," Edward whispered, "I doubt anyone at Scotland Yard would be able to locate you for prosecution."

"This young lady is stronger than she looks," she said. "I think she will recover."

"Louisiana?" Doctor Wainsford said behind Edward. "How's the young patient fairing?"

"Better than she looked a few minutes ago," she said. "Just look."

The doctor felt the girl's cheeks then her neck. He placed his stethoscope to her chest and listened. He then looked at detective Willoughby.

"My apologies, Detective," He said. "Your intervention saved this little girl. You were at the garment factory fires?"

"From beginning to end." Edward said.

"Then you are a better judge of this type of situation than me."

"Hardly. I'm just stubborn."

"I'll leave this young girl in both your and Louisiana's capable hands," Doctor Wainsford looked at the cages. "I have other patients to tend to."

"Off you go, doctor," Edward said. "I'll inform you if the situation changes here."

"She's near the same age as my Susan." Franklin patted the matted hair. His huge hands seemed out of place, yet with a softness Edward had never before seen. "Don't worry, my sweet. You are safe now. No one will ever 'urt you again.

"We need to get these bastards," Franklin whispered to Edward.

"We will." Edward looked up at Louisiana. "Do you need anything, madam?"

"No, Detective." She dipped the cloth back in the bowl of water. "Right now, she needs water. Everything else is secondary. I will clean her up later. Clara, fetch a comb and a brush from my bedroom and go to Sandra's room and see if we have any clothes which will fit this young girl."

"Yes, mum," and Clara headed out into the basement of the house.

"Detective?" Louisiana said.

"Yes, madam?" Edward looked at the woman's strained face.

"Go detect. Build your case. I am certain my husband did not act alone. Catch these animals. I will help you in any way I can." She locked eyes with Edward. "Go."

"Yes, madam. Keep me posted as to this one's situation."

"I will."

"Franklin, fetch Cadet Peterson, and we'll begin organizing the evidence."

"On it," and Franklin trotted off to find the cadet.

23 February 1892, 1800:

The hours ticked off, and patient after patient was evacuated from the underground prison. Half a dozen were already dead, and they were being prepared for transport to Scotland Yard's morgue.

"Detective Willoughby," Coroner Waddington looked over his wire-rimmed glasses.

"Coroner Waddington," Edward said. "How goes your investigation?"

"It appears our cases are intertwined once more. Six dead so far and three more who might not see daybreak." He looked about the room. "How can you stand the smell?"

"It's not easy, sir. We're almost finished with our initial collection; then we will breath free air once more."

"What do you need from me?"

"Confirmation that these people were being used to determine the effect of the opium. I believe they were no more than lab rats to Neville Garner."

"I'll give you that confirmation right now, Detective. All the dead were given lethal doses of the narcotic."

"I'll have the living tested," Doctor Wainsford said. "If they're addicted, then we have more work to do."

"Were there any needle marks on the young girl?" Edward said.

"None that I could find," Wainsford said. "Perhaps she was spared that horror. Time will tell."

"Thank you doctor," Edward said. "We'll be off to Scotland Yard soon to put a case together."

"Bad news, I'm afraid on that front, Edward," Coroner Waddington said. "It seems Neville Garner was released just minutes before your message arrived."

"Damn! My concern," Edward said, "is our contract killer gets to him first. I believe we will be looking for a body and not a living suspect."

"Good riddance," Franklin said. "I know you wanted to question him, Edward, but if 'e's already dead, the world will be a better place."

"Amen," Cadet Peterson said.

"I concur with both of you," Cadet Brown said.

23 February 1892, 1900:

Valeria Kaprianov arrived at the Garner residence at the request of Detective Willoughby. She would translate for many of the patients, who were Russian or Ukrainian immigrants.

She whispered to the young girl, now resting comfortably on a luxurious bed in the Garner residence.

"Her name is Elena Oleg Pakhomov," Valeriya sighed. "She is Ukrainian, from Myronivka, near Shostka, a mining town. Her mother is one of the dead in the prison. She has no other family."

"Well, Valeriya," Louisiana said. "She does now."

Seventeen

Neville Garner approached the docks. He had arranged passage on a freighter with a destination of Savannah, Georgia in the United States. It was due to debark in just two hours, and he wanted to embark just prior to casting off.

He studied the immediate area, the fog billowing across the Thames, and did not see any policemen anywhere. He pulled back into the alley for a brief respite, so he would look fresh upon arrival. A shadow moved behind him and he never saw the hand with the blade perform a lightning-speed swipe across his throat.

"For my children," was all the killer said. When the body crumpled to the pavement, he placed a note on the dead man's chest.

24 February 1892, 0300:

"Right this way, sir," the Bobbie said. "We left the body untouched when we saw the note."

Edward and Robert bent over the body, cadets Brown and Peterson looking on. The note was a familiar one:

```
For Detective Edward Willoughby
```

Edward's gloved fingers picked up the envelope and he sniffed it. Without any obvious danger, he opened it. The note read:

```
            Justice Served.
        This is not over.
```

ABOUT THE AUTHOR

Tim Lewis is a former U.S. Navy Journalist and reporter for a small weekly newspaper. He has been writing for most of his adult life, but literary accomplishments have come within the past few years. He has many works in progress in several genres, and Murder in Dartmouth Park is his second novella in the Edward Willoughby series.

Look for Murder in Queen's Park, coming soon.